GW01451303

FIREFLIES IN THE CITY

Ariq.

Copyright © *Ariq* . 2020

This edition was first published in 2020.

All rights reserved. No part of this publication may be reproduced, stored in a retrieval system, or transmitted, in any form or by any means, electronic, mechanical, photocopying, recording or otherwise, without the prior permission of the copyright owner.

This is a work of fiction. Names, places, characters, and incidents are either the product of the author's imagination or are used fictitiously. Any resemblance to any actual persons, living or dead, or events, is purely coincidental.

ISBN 979-8-67293-047-3

Imprint: Independently published

For London, and its many streets that rip you to shreds and the other streets that help you find the pieces.

'Mother says'– she hesitated uncertainly –
'Mother says that two souls are sometimes
created together and – and in love before they're
even born.'

F. Scott Fitzgerald,

The Beautiful and the Damned

Fireflies in the City

Part One: Starry Nights.

Transport Amnesia.
Spitalfields.
Candy Girl.
Ecstasy.
Eternal Youth.
Outlines.
Picture Frames.
Fake Destines

Part Two: The Renaissance.

Aisles of Fear.
Northern Loneliness.
Orbit.
Night Trains.
Slight Smirks.
Constellations.
Caller from London.

Part Three: Vive le Chagrin.

Watered Tragedies.
Raindrops.
Little Venice.
Foreign Souls.
One-way Ticket.
Soft Wails.

PART ONE:

STARRY NIGHTS.

Transport Amnesia.

The music drowns out, the soft hum of breathing dies and the world slows. Suddenly I am afraid of the amnesia that will kick in tonight: that I will forget how her skin glows under the lights, forget how her nose has a soft bump on its bridge, forget that her eyes glow like lights on aeroplane wings in the dead sky. Premature neediness courses through my body.

Apologies are in order. We have not introduced ourselves; she exists nameless, remembered by the soft pearls she bares when staring at her phone. We have not had any daily conversations where we complain about the harsh realities of life. We have nothing - all we have is a brief moment where our eyes lock and the spark begins to grow. An inferno within the heart yet moments later our fires are extinguished by a woman in a trench coat blocking my view.

She shifts: she wants to be seen. She wants to see me.
Timid smiles shared as we both rest our heads on the glass pane opposite each other. Who is she? Who are we? Will we ever know?

The world comes to an instant halt. The music will never return and the rest of the passengers have disappeared. We are the last people in existence. If the world was ending, I would move to sit next to her. We would sit in silence but at least with the knowledge of who we are: nobody; somebody; everybody. We go from being strangers to the last stars that illuminate the way for lost tourists in the polluted canvas above.

The other passengers return to life as the train halts and I watch her stand to leave. My heart rate rises instinctively as the heel steps onto the platform. As the train jolts to restart its journey, we watch each other through the window.
Soft smiles.

The music returns.

Spitalfields.

We seem almost desperate to find each other. Our cold hearts even more glacial under the city lights which beat in unison, pumping the blood around the bodies of the towering office blocks. We are so connected yet I have lost her. The existence of her Irish green coat merely a memory - alas, I cannot remember all of her.

I weave through the stalls that form the market and sometimes I surmise that I see her. Was it the same woman who walked out of Chanel Beauty? Was it the same woman who bumped into a coffee table? And was it the same woman who smiled when she saw the 'hat man' standing at his relatively unpopular stall? I long for it to be - but only because I pray for the chance to pluck up the courage and brush past her - like the blade that carves fruit.

As I collect my coffee and question why I buy things I don't like, she sees me. It is a glance - a short one - but nonetheless being noticed once more is flattering. The giddiness once experienced is painfully short: the coffee has begun to burn my palm.

My face shifts in her direction, similar to a sunflower turning to its master. Her glances are now stares, and for once discomfort is not on my agenda. There is a magnetic attraction that propels my feet to walk in the direction of my muse; I halt a metre in. Is this the wrong thing? The wrong moment? The wrong girl? Am I out of order?

I cannot tell if the corners of her mouth rise, the lack of polish on my shoes is suddenly far more engrossing. There is the sound of a heel piercing the ground - it comes from in front.

An arm is extended and a hand placed on my shoulder. I look up.
She grins.
"Hello."

Candy Girl.

Crushed velvet coats her voice.
It embraces me, it's tenor sweeter than candy.
Syllables drowned in cocoa.

Ask me questions. Ask me what my name is.
Ask me what it is I do everyday. Ask me who I
am.
Can I answer all of those? Can I?

The soft curl of her tongue when she says
certain words is a reminder of how a child
wraps their own around a lollipop.
Her cheeks are full, it gives her a soft quality.
Soft - everything is soft: her voice, her gaze, the
atmosphere around us that no longer cuts away
at our gummy dreams of seeing each other a
second time.

The crackle of our reignited fires carries both
joy and fear. She will get my hopes high. I'm
sure of it. Which one of us will take the other
for granted? Will she crush my cola bottle heart,
or will it be hers that is ripped between the sharp
teeth that eat away at our longing?

Even so, still I stand before her. Chasing
destiny.
Her cheeks flush London red. Bright red: like
conversation hearts.

Sweethearts.

Our eyes are fixated on each other. Are we crossing any lines? Any roads? What territory is this? Whose world is this?

I'll blame it on my nerves that my voice cracks when I ask her for her name.
She grins.
"Rosie."
Rosalie. Rosie. Rose. Red like cartoon hearts.
Red like apples. Is she my downfall?
But for now: red like strawberry laces.

Ecstasy.

One heartbeat. Unity under the glow of the lamp
that sits on the bedside table.
The blinds remain open and the stars of the city
landscape highlight her picture.
Aphrodite's offspring - her mother is her muse.
The fatality in her alluring voice potent.
Regardless, she shifts in pleasure.

Unfamiliar highs stress my mind as my fingers
trace the arches in her body.
The tempo rises as does my breathing.
The skies begin to shift as she reaches to press
her palm against my cheek. Flattery.
Her breathing has quickened. Flattery.
It's these nights that I congratulate myself on
even looking up from my phone that day on the
train.

Shattered movements. Broken kisses.
The moans of ecstasy beat those of a morphine-
fuelled high. A new drug discovery and the
amount of trials she's been through doesn't
affect me.
Call me selfish, but now we belong to each
other. No one else.

Tomorrow, she will rise from interrupted
slumber and only smile at me. Gathering her

belongings, she will slip away, perhaps after leaving her number on a tissue in the kitchen.
It will become a Sunday morning ritual.
The same way these shared sensual moments will become our Saturday night prayers.

Sprawled all over the floor: her clothes, my clothes and any self-doubt.
Closing my eyes, I let her press her lips against my own. It's an open invitation.
Call me needy. Call me lonely. I crave to be held.
She says she wants me - an unspoken invocation for her to tell me she needs me.

Stolen moments. Precious memories. Twisted emotions.
From transport lovers to clay models - we mould our bodies for maximum pleasure.
Call my name.
And watch me whisper hers.

My hopes hike upwards. She lays there, her arms wrapped around me.
I want her to want me.
Breathe.
I want her to need me.
Breathe.
I want her to remember my name.

Sugar crush.

Chocolate glazed skies.
Petal covered gardens.
Saccharine honey coats my tongue.

"Rosie?"
"Yeah?" Her voice faint as our individual galaxies begin to fuse.
"Hold me." A guise of supplication.
"Okay."

Dewy-eyed ecstasy.

Eternal Youth.

We sip on plastic straws.
No care for the effect it will have on the
environment in years to come, because as we sit
under the cracked sky, we question whether we
will live to see tomorrow.
The rain begins to decorate the objects below
and loosen the sins that stick to us: water of
purity.
The clouds pity us.
"Quench their thirst." The cumulus' say to each
other.

We sit on roofs that need repairing, smoking
cigarettes and kissing the droplets with our once
virgin lips. We long to become one with our
universe.
I feel young and dumb. I have missed this.
The wind drastically increases in speed.

"Blow them off the roof," one particle says to
the other, "Blow their tragedies away."
Nature pities us; it is unexplored territory. I am
grateful to be the victim of the Mother Nature's
thoughts.

The wind caresses my skin, making its way
through the gaps it finds between my flesh and
the fabric I don. If the breeze comes to a halt,
may it halt my heart with it; for I sit, leaning

back, my elbows resting on roof tiles. I scan the grey ceiling under the harsh conditions - and I see colour.

Stop my heart and cement my destiny. I turn to face Rosie by my side, her eyes are closed. She - with me - welcomes the rain. It cleanses her face and as her skin absorbs it - her heart too.

Immature, juvenile, childlike.

Stop my heart and carry my woes away with the final gust.

Let me not be known for my lack of accomplishments not my struggles. Because within these moments, as the wind strips me of any signs of maturation, my issues cease to be of any bother.

If the wind stops in unison with my pacemaker, then may I find the tranquillity that I longed to find here.

A queer thought laces through my mind: I have already found my peace, the breeze has put me at ease with life.

Alas, the breeze stops. My heart does not. I begin to cherish the return of the warm, stale air: it means life is back to normal. Though now, all I can think of is the peace I felt moments ago.

Is it fear that wants the breeze back?

Fear of what is to come?

No, it can't be.

The signs of ageing launch their arrival journey.
"Bring the breeze back." I turn to the sky.
Nature sympathises with my sorrow: the winds slowly begins to build once more.

If she, beside me, wakes to find me numb and no more; may she see a man of good makeup.
May she see me in my eternal youth.
If she wakes to find me sitting up, blowing rings from cigarette smoke, may she see a man of tender heart.
May she see me in my eternal youth.

Outlines.

Palm against the horn, I press down on it; to no avail, the traffic remains to be stationary.

"Relax," she has the grin of a toddler. "It's not like we need to rush."

There are many things wrong with her statement, one being the fact that if we reach our destination too late in the day, then we reduce the invaluable memories we could make.

"Don't you want to have fun?" Genuinely addled, I ask in order to decipher whether or not this trip is a waste of time.

"Of course I do but we can have fun in the car." Is that a point riddled with sexual connotations? I don't answer: the traffic is moving.

She sips her cappuccino, "It's just Brighton."

I laugh, a little hurt; Brighton is my favourite place in the world. The ragged rocks that are smoothed by attrition; the smell of cheap beer that floats around the shore; the vintage record shops, like Shoreditch by the sea. I don't let her know of my feelings: there's no point.

I've never taken a woman on a journey before, though I suppose Rosie deserves it, her Geordie soul has apparently only visited two cities: Newcastle and London.

"My dad didn't believe that the U.K. had other places." Her mouth moves slowly.

"He has seen a map, right?" The real question is; does he know Edinburgh exists?

We spend the next hour talking about Brighton and everything it has to offer. I speak about my initial disappointment when the realisation that it was a beach made of rocks and not sand slapped me across the face; the Royal Pavilion and the fact its architecture is an imitation of the Taj Mahal; and the Lanes.

"It's actually quite a nice place to be, fucking beautiful if I'm being honest." The grin etched onto my face is harsh, she notices it and smiles.

"Why's it so special? Come on, let's have a deep conversation." There's something about making the point of wanting a deep conversation which makes it redundant.

"I had my first date in Brighton," to say I'm a liar would be a false statement in itself. "She went to Brighton College and was the friend of a friend."

Did I want Rosie to be vexed that I had brought up the mention of another girl? Then again, schoolyard affairs are barely controlled by the mind, let alone the heart.

"What was her name?"

"Orla."

Orla: the first thing I noticed about her was her earrings. They were shaped like little glass bottles, and on closer inspection I recognised the paper label of cola. Her soft features were framed by her cropped blonde bob cut, with her hairs flying in the wind with every step she would take past me.

We met at a friend's eighteenth birthday party in Brighton; she was the first person aside from said friend and I to be sitting at the designated meet-up location. I knew it was because she was a local to the area - her journey wasn't as time consuming as the others who were all travelling using the Thameslink trains.

My attraction towards her grew not only due to her dedication to be punctual but also due to the fact she raised the first valid point of the day, "Why didn't you all travel together?"

Her question was directed at me - she could not quiz the birthday boy (that would invalidate social rules) - I fumbled in coming to a concrete answer.

"They're lazy." My intonation resulted in the statement resonating as a question, with the way my voice raised at the penultimate word.

It terminated with her first smile of our three-month courtship.

There is internal debate on whether our first meeting at the party can be counted as a first date. My decision is not final, though it is a 'yes'. Still one of the days which remains vividly in my withering memory, it trumps all other first

*dates. We walked the shore with our shoes held
between the fingers of the hand that were
furthest away from each other, my other hand
was intertwined with hers. Her fingers were
freakishly long and she would run them through
her conditioned hair every time nerves would
conquer her emotions.*

*The first time my lips pressed those of another
person was that very night; we stood in a vinyl
shop in North Laine pretending that we
understood and cherished the Bee Gees, instead
as we stood on stained carpet, we cherished
each other. Raw passion radiating off of two
teenagers: both equally as lost in life.*

Kisses of life killing the reluctance to live.

Rosie stares at me as I recount the complete
story of my novelty of an affair at seventeen.
"You kissed her in a record shop?" Why is that
the only thing in her mind?
"Yeah."
"Oh," cue the prolonged pause. Is there an issue
with records? "So, you listen to records?"
"Urm. No." Although, I've always wanted to
buy a record player and become one of those
men who stock up on vinyl records and play
each record expressing how much more
'authentic' it is. I have not yet arrived at that
destination. "I don't even own a record player."

The reasoning behind standing in the record shop was that the rain had started and was heavy. Aphrodite was crying tears of her happiness: her most pathetic child had experienced his first act of passion.

"I'll buy you one." The only music I want to hear is her tune of her voice. Endless notes of infatuation.

The cars continue to move along the A23, a view from above would make us look like a long line of dots - 'Cut here.'

Girls Aloud sing to the beat of the movement of my car. Today will be a good day.

The rest of the journey, she spends asking about my upbringing and family, I carefully omit specific details.

"Who is your favourite ex?" The questions are beginning to pry. I like it - she's making an effort to get to know me.

Small moment and small questions, all pit stops on the path to eternal love.

"Carys."

Carys: a prime model of her name. The root 'caru' being the Welsh word for 'love'. Her desirability led to the first time I tasted the stupefied feelings of an orgasm.

We were not the smartest pairing, but we were the most jovial. The banes of life did not phase Carys, for she so loved the world that in her eyes it could do her no wrong. When an issue would arise, her ability to love would bring yesterday back around and happiness would return. The touches of the pressure she could apply to the curvatures of my body made her my intoxicant.

It was on my nineteenth birthday when she lunged for me, gripping each side of my unbuttoned trench coat. To stand on the green lawn outside our accommodation was impermissible; young rebellion, break the rules but fix the puzzle of sensuality.

My room was decorated with multicoloured string lights, film posters, old train tickets and magazine cut-outs. She had been in my room before, though this must have been the moment where she absorbed her surroundings. The common theory is that during a wave of lustful sex, everything is rapid and fast paced - that is false. Time paces on at a more leisurely stride and colours become more vibrant, outlines sharper and pictures brighter - the removal of cataracts.

She undressed me first, taking her manicured nails and unbuttoning my plaid shirt with care.

"Let's do this." It was more a statement to prepare herself than to alert me of my next move.

Groans of rapture released from my larynx as she ran the tips of her nails over the perimeter of my inguinal crease.

I stood there nude as she allowed me to fumble with the straps of her dress. There was no pressure to perform well, though I could hardly speak with my nerves becoming overbearing.

We made no explicit choices that night, but we made our greatest choices. The streetlamps lit up with every moment that my moans rose in octave, we sang in harmony; born from our labour was a standard that would be forever unmatched by any other woman.

Carys, my first lover. Carys, my first woman. Carys, my first love. The misery our parting brought me was severe, so why do it? She was my first addiction. Necessity was the only word to describe my want for her; to shower me with affection and lash out when she didn't. An unhealthy dependency and it all filtered down to my issues. To say my heart still doesn't call Carys' name on a lonely night would have to result in having my tongue severed for speaking fiction.

It's a useless attempt to forget Carys that my attention relaxes upon Rosalie.

"Those are pretty earrings." I say, turning my gaze to the way she sits.

"Eyes on the road, please." She seems irate. Is it my fault? Was it wrong to mention Carys?

"Do you still love her?" Her timbre is resentful.

Orla hadn't seemed to be an issue. I'm sure I spoke of both women in the same way.

I am not a liar.

I am not an actor.

However, I am not going to cut the threads that have formed between us over these past few weeks.

I turn the music up.

Picture Frames.

She wants me to do the right thing even though I have no clue what that is.

"Why'd you have to fucking do that?" Her tone is harsh. Any harsher and there won't be any depth left for the wound to deepen.

"Do what?" Don't think I'm playing an ignorant role - I am truly perplexed.

She stares me down.

Once upon a time we danced with movie stars in our imagination. Tonight, she speaks to me as if I am the villain in our short film. Fear courses through my veins, the red of my blood tinting an undiscovered shade of blue.

Close my eyes and set fire to the furniture around me. Her immaturity already damaging the world we have built together in such a minute space of time - it's only fair that I get my turn at this. I rip off the wallpaper we hung together in my mind, like adhesive plasters covering the punctures of a once cracked heart. The pain we feel differs drastically: she doesn't seem to care. Maybe she thinks the same of my reactions.

"Why do you always have to be so dramatic?" Venom laces my pauses.

My words are the gas to the flame of pure fury. Her eruption is almost magnificent to watch, an always active volcano having its most drastic eruption. A swan song till it becomes dormant. A swan song for our courtship?

"Maybe if you listened," her tears like a stream that could satisfy the cravings of the flowers in a drought; flowers that no longer grow between us. Now we merely allow weeds and shrubbery to spring from the crevices of our once shared mystery. "If you listened to me, we could be happy."

Listen. Pay attention. Take a mental note of every word. What is there to listen to? The music is dead. Once so in tune, the pegs of her guitar twisted by fate, and I watched from my piano as the strings of both our instruments fractured. No shared notes. We played broken chords in sabotaged keys - our mistakes silenced by the applause of those who knew us.

"I do listen." My voice is calm whilst I recite my line.

Her blue eyes (contemporarily indigo with sorrow) stare back at me bewildered.

"You do not!" I flinch at her raised voice but shun the childhood memories that are starting to resurface. "You never do what I ask you to. You never do what I say!"

I question her level of maturity - she wants to be in charge in an almost puerile way. When we dressed this morning, I thought we wore the same trousers, just sharing one leg each. Alas, she wore a pair of harsh jeans that my eyes and heart are foreign to.

A longing for my tears to come disappears. The want to show her that this relationship equates to my entity, disappears. There is no valid reason for crying tears of false nature: crocodile tears.

We are and will always be a beautiful creation, mesmerising by the way our bodies caress each other under golden sunsets and silver twilights. Yet, I begin to question the nature of the sparks we create. Are we only diamonds due to the pressure we've been put under? Or were we diamonds beforehand? Instinct points towards the former idea.

Faded Polaroid prints have festooned her walls, there is no set formation. They're stuck on randomly - I can see the grainy outlines of my face in some of the pictures. Donning the wall like a firework - it is explosive. It's in her nature. It's deep within my own too.
You're not like him. I think to myself. I pray that I'm not like him.

Who is 'him'? At this point it no longer matters, he's already made his impact on me, and I watch the effects come to life.

"Why do you have to be so difficult?" My voice is condescending - I can hear the parent-child tone on my voice. I hate it but I like how it rips away at her even more. Maybe it is the dominance it gives me; that I am the one who is able to anger her to this foreign level. Uncharted even for her.
"How am I the difficult one?" Stretched syllables. "Tell me how!"
I don't answer.

She is in the kitchen. The noise of her rustling around the pantry fill the rest of the apartment - the diffusion of sound - from high concentration to low concentration; only her eating whittles away at the silence. She is looking for something else to snack on, the sudden absence of clamour a strong indication; we constantly search for different things. She searches for chocolates to cushion the pain she feels in the moment, yet I search for conclusions.

My eyes follow the way her skirt shifts in the air as she walks towards me. I can sense the fact that she is preparing herself to apologise; it irritates me slightly – our issues have not been resolved. A twisted reaction: I do not want her to eat her words. It's pathetic that I think that I have twisted her cogs the opposite way for her to portray such an alien emotion; it is also immature that I want to make amends first in order to hold a better position. Could it be that the only reason she wants to apologise is to have one-upped me too?

"Leave me alone." My words like saws and picks sharp enough to sculpt an ice statue of Snedronningen.
Her stance matches that of a crocodile ultimately questioning whether eating its prey is the most sensible.
"Fuck off." Once acid to my ears, now it is an essential oil – it brings me pleasure.
She has made a vain attempt to wear the coat of a female alpha, the same way she tried to wear the pants of this relationship; I rip the pride away from her.
Am I afraid of her possession of power? No.
But do I want to be on the same level? Yes.
Do I want us to see our world and our issues with the same eyes? Yes.

"Get out of my house," Trembles. "Get out!"
Please cry. Is it sick that I find so much joy in her pain? I justify my sadistic behaviour by questioning the candour of her pain as well as explaining to myself that this is revenge – she's

hurt me before. Is she truly hurt? Am I overreacting?

My legs are close to giving away - weakness. However, I make it to the door with great pride. I'm twisted. I'm fucked up. With great pity, I prove that I feel no guilt and I love it. My fingers trace the craft tape that sticks a picture on the wall and I carefully remove it.
She watches me perplexed. She questions if I still care.
I put it in my pocket and without turning back to give her a soft smile, I walk out the door.

I wanted fireplaces not fireworks. Love not shallow passion. I wanted what the world is struggling to give me: I can either stay and force the hand of the universe or I can find it elsewhere.

The laces of hope have been untied. Now they form a noose around my neck preparing me for death.
Red like apples. Is she my downfall?
Yes.
Hung, drawn and quartered: and a picture of my mutilation will one day grace her wall.

Fake Destinies.

We both knew that our agreement was
temporary.
She should have known that I was temporary.
It is purposeless to act like we have to hide the
missiles that fulminate in our minds.
She stares at me, the vapour of false promises
like lavender.

Of late, my emotions have been in constant
drive. You tell me it's because I'm a Pisces yet
in reality, it's because I miss driving a stick
through our shared misery.
Control. Dominance. Command.

She says that I say 'sorry' a great deal.
"It's intolerable. Stop apologising."
"Sorry."
What more can I say?
I wasn't born to fuck up her heart.

I've been a silent death.
She can comb my hair, rest her head on my
shoulder, even smile.
Nonetheless my slaughter has now aged.
Now I'm out of time. We are out of time.

"Say you love me." She begs.
My fingers twirl a strand of her hair before
tucking it behind her ear.

"Say it to my face." Another plead.
Does she need to hear it once more? Or is it
unethical to utter words with no substance? No
truth.
Silence. Having become a being with no soul:
silence.

This romance has grated away at me, so why do
I contemplate quitting her?
Ketamine to my youthful heart. We were
supposed to run wild.
The transformation into a brigand of our future
is painful. Requisite all the same.

Chained to the ride we built together.
Screams of adrenaline glazed with newfound
desolation.
We tire of donning feigned smiles.
Who have we become?

She cups my chin between her once tender
fingers. The nails have been carved for murder.
"Do you love me?"
It's old blood now.
An extinguished blaze.
A tempestuous affair of the heart.
"No."

The sugar begins to rot my teeth.
"What?" Synthetic softness.
There will be no oaths on reactions.

I am not an actor. Fuck a fake destiny.
"No."

PART TWO:

THE RENAISSANCE.

Aisles of Fear.

Projections on white bed sheets. We wanted flat sheets nonetheless our fates were blanketed with fitted ones: we had to compromise. It is a slow independent movie, the budget is low, but the laughs are high, the colours are muted yet vibrant. Winter woes. Summer sorrow. The characters are filled with dried passion. Who are they? I watch my face appear on the projector. It's us. Alas, there is no 'us'. Not anymore. No longer is she the woman who craved the touch of my nether lip. Rosalie: a blood flower decomposing under the soil of new beginnings.

The slight vibration of my phone pressed against my upper thigh wakes me from my daze. My fingers are delicate as I slip it out: delicacy for the wrong object; soft now, yet vicious on hearts.
The notification is from a friend, an invitation to spend the night getting drunk and high, 'throw myself in the deep end'.
And will I struggle to come back to the surface?
Yes.
On any other day, I would gladly accept the summon to bathe in the scent of sweet juices and floral perfumes. Though today, my body

feels drained of any energy that it once harboured.

I don't respond to the text, not because I'm too tired to type the letters 'n' and 'o' but rather because I'm still unsure. I am aware of my own behaviour: if I lose myself tonight, I lose myself forever. It's almost poetic - getting intoxicated under club lights for a string of continuous days - the way the world begins to stop having an effect on a person. Under multicoloured lights, the world begins to stop existing.

Can it also be granted as poetic that I come to these conclusions whilst standing in a supermarket cereal aisle? The answer is subjective. Nonetheless, there I stand, body erect, my feet drilled into the ground like the shelves on the walls.

"Excuse me." She seems apologetic that she wants me to shift.
I stare back incredulously, not sure what she wants exactly, she points at the variety of cereal that my shopping trolley blocks.
"Sorry." I push my cart forwards and turn back to see her carefully take a box of 'Crunchy Nut'.
"Is that the biggest size?" His voice is the correct counterpart to his features: a low timbre for a man with a rugged complexion.

She hands him the box and smiles. "Yeah, yeah it is." He smiles back.

It's sickening; like syrup made from the wrong sugars. My inner biome waters the plant of resent: *fuck them. It won't last.* Just as it didn't last for Rosie and myself; my spiteful nature, wants others to experience my pain.

The sound of an announcement for a staff member to go to the tills brings me back to sanity. The couple has disappeared back to their mundane life and left me all alone once more. I wonder what they do in the spare time. He looks like the sort of man who enjoy going to a Wetherspoons to watch the match, he radiates the stench of Guinness and cigarettes. She looks like the kind of woman who likes to sit on her faux leather couch opposite the tv and flick through multiple channels.

"Why did the Jeremy Kyle Show have to get cancelled?" I can almost hear her say it through the phone on a rainy day.

So many questions for people whose names I've not been granted the knowledge of.

With every step I take away from the cereal aisle, I begin to let them go, allow them to disappear. To think, a man and a woman whose faces I have already forgotten, have clung to my mind for longer than what is sensible.

The aisle with shelves stacked with juices and soft drinks of all flavours, is occupied by multiple families. There is a child crying in one corner whose walls are supported by that of another child in the opposite corner. The disorder, the mess, the disarray of it all is almost comedic. One of the crying children slowly climbs into his father's arms and rests his growing head on his shoulder.

The fragility of children is what has always drawn me to the idea of becoming a parent: a future I saw with my Rosie. I would sow seeds and she would tend to them, though we would both watch them grow. The youth are confusing creations with their mood swings being almost bipolar. The child in his father's arms has stopped crying, now his high-pitched laugh spreads throughout the surrounding area. The giggles are a form of fresh torture, I can't help but wonder if my child would snigger with me the same way.

"Where's mummy?" My child would ask.
"She's gone - gone away." She'll have moved on by now, I'm sure of it, she is relatively quick regarding these matters. How do you tell your imaginary infant that 'mummy' doesn't love me anymore?
"Do you still love mummy?" He asks me, his lips against my ear.

Bile appears to be stuck in my throat and my breathing begins to take form of a twisted pace. Do I love Rosie? Did I love Rosie?
"Don't ask stupid questions." And the child disappears, just like he did when I parted with my northern jewel. It could be due to the fact he asks so many questions, I don't want to see him return.

Once again, I snap back to reality and stand in an empty aisle. Is this insanity? This longing for a woman I so quickly let go of? Do I crave her touch, a finale to our escapades, or do I yearn the touch of anyone willing to show me attention and affection? Solitude, a curse placed upon the world by Hades, a perverted method of sharing perdition with the broken creations of Gaia's dissolving earth.

To purchase nothing and leave a store is embarrassing, yet at this point in my career, I no longer care for the judgment of others. Now, I only care for: devotion, intimacy and lust, all coated in the hard shell of tenderness. I long for it, and it will be mine. I want it. I need it. I can see it.
Far in the distance, I can see the blinding lights of an ambulance van, like the flashes within a disco. Intensity, hunger, zeal; all float between the minute gaps of bodies grinding against each other.

Pressing the keys on my phone, I type out a basic text that if read by anybody else would be seen as effortless. Only I know of the ache it brings to my hub and only I know of the concealed joy within – the chance to meet new people. New characters. New nymphs. New loves.

His response is just as simple as my original text: 'See you there.'
The lights wake up in my core.

Northern Loneliness.

It's not easy preparing for a night out –
regardless of gender. For some reason all the
past mistakes I've ever made always come
flooding back to me as I step into clean jeans.
Mistakes. Memories. Decisions.

I left my family at eighteen.
Never to return, on my heels, I disappeared like
a doe running from a lion.
I ran and never turned back, like an immigrant
leaving his native country to start a new life.
I ran and never turned back, like a man whose
soul was being taken to the afterlife.

We were not a compatible grouping. Having
grown up the bottom of the food chain, I was
painted with the idea that I would be cherished,
alas, that was not the case.

At the age of fifteen, I decided to start voicing
my own opinions much to my mother's avail
and annoyance. Our conversations were born
from angry taunts and lack of mutual
understanding. Once destined to be great
friends, we were punished with becoming
enemies of differing beliefs.

My father was purely an acquaintance of mine;
we spoke rarely and when we did it either

resolved with me being subject to his foolish remarks or a quiet greeting. The lack of relationship that we split between us made it easier for me to dissipate from his existence and he - generally - from mine. As the days were slowly being counted and ticked on my calendar, a small portion of me wanted to reach out to him. I prayed that he would take me as who I was and watch me ascend to his throne. Still, he never branched out to me, so I took my olives and faded into obscurity.

Parting with my siblings was vastly more arduous; so difficult in fact, that I still see them on rare occasions. Whilst we never built relationships that could be seen from the window seat of a plane, our connections were established with strong foundations. They've watched me grow up; I've watched them grow as people; I've watched their children grow from newborns to toddlers. A hidden friendship, no matter how many times we attempt to turn away from each other.

"We can't see each other anymore." One of them once said to me under the hanging lights of a restaurant in Southwark.
"Why?" It's ironic - I was the one who made the aim to kill my character in their stories yet I'm always the one whose world collapses when we part.

"They don't want us to," 'They' was a collective reference to my parents. "You left - that was your choice. Why keep in contact?" Silence. My mouth could not open. My voice could not be heard, though the screams were high pitched and furious in my head.

When I left, I only ever wanted to leave the structure of the society my family had built, to leave the destructive elements of the culture I was born into. My parents embodied our culture and so beautiful it could have been should they have been created of anything but its flaws. My siblings saw those flaws in euphoric image my parents had printed - it was the link of the chain that clasped us together.

"I left them. I left it all. I didn't want to leave you guys."

"But you did." That was the last time I saw that specific sibling. To bring myself to bear the sadness that seeing their face would bring has no worth.

I never ran; I didn't disintegrate one night with or without leaving a note; I stuck it out until the last day. My mother was adamant that I either studied in London or gave up on my education, her overbearing nature made me crave to enter the outside world even more than usual.

When it came time to apply to different universities, I made all of my choices outside of

London - the further north the better. Sending my application off knowing that if I was accepted into any university it would be away from my personal hell was a form of catharsis.

When I received my grades and acceptance letter, I prayed that my heart would silently crack. *You're leaving your family behind.* It didn't. My heart couldn't even lie to my mind and tell it that remote sadness would have been sensible. At university, my droughts of human interaction would leave me despondent. Finding the hope to keep moving relied on remembering that whilst the present was a malediction, the future was going to be a gift. And it has been, I see the joy in all that I have loved: my first apartment, Diana, Rosalie. I allow the memory of her voice to linger for a few seconds too long. In a new way I'm back to the start: lonely. Alone when I moved out. Alone when I lost Rosalie. Destined to be alone - a reflection of my parents.

The lack of regret sickens me. What if my own child left me all alone? There was a reason propelling every one of my actions; but were they truly warranted? And as I sit on the train towards Morden; on the journey back to the damp apartment that no longer feels like home - I pledge to myself that I shall never turn out like my ancestors. Streams of tears cried at canals

and in therapy chairs, "You are not your father",
the statement has value. I take the penknife that
hangs from my keyring and press the blade into
my palm with gentle pressure. The skin
separates as the mild current of blood fills my
cupped hand: cleansing my body - cleansing my
world.

Some mistakes get made.
Some curses do get prayed.
Never to return: feel my hurt, feel my pain,
And the message of my agony is that I'm alone
and drained,
And I think I'm going to go insane.

Orbit.

Mercury: needles pierce our skin; we inject the happiness that once belonged only to the galaxy. The club lights are alive, and the dancers are awake. There hangs a tacky disco ball from the ceiling - maybe it's for comedic effect – maybe it's a forgotten memory of the eighties.
Whatever the reason it hangs from the ceiling, the gleams it emits bring me back to the tip I've just pressed into my veins. Let me be vigorous and not indolent.
Give me more.
Let me become one with my sun and stars.
Let me become the sun.

Venus: her body moves like the wind. Fierce twists; elegance on her heel yet anger screams through her flailing arms. She is going under. Who has hurt her? Will she ever be pulled out?

Earth: the fermented rye fills her body. Her new blood - it paces through her veins, bringing destruction with her with every movement. She is not broken yet her eyes are lost. Alive but not living. The people around make her anxious - the sweat begins to slowly secrete. A clammy palm presses against my own, our sweat intermingles. Both afraid but in fear together. Is this confidence?

Mars: he speaks little yet his soul speaks of tales beyond this basement. How he remembers a world where the glow of the sun or midnight moon can caress him, I do not know. All I know of are club lights and photo booths. When I stare at his imperfect features, it is laced with jealousy for he can remember a world I cannot. He can go back to his universe whilst I cannot. So different yet so similar. Alas, all I can bring myself to say to him is, "Take a picture with me."

Jupiter: golden glares. His passion for life is evident from the way he cries aloud, his ability to move his mouth in unison with the lyrics playing in the room is a talent. We all watch him, others think that he hasn't noticed our stares: on the contrary, he stares back at us discretely. Dancing alone is a form of beauty, the way he does it: it is transcendent. He is out of control but his clutch on our stares keeps him grounded.
Broken beats. Guilty feet. He floats away.

Saturn: her hips revolve around endlessly. The rhythm courses through her, encapsulating her energy. Who is she? Where has she come from?
Her slight tan is complimented by the glow of the lights: she is alight. The rings on her fingers attack each other and cause what might be the

most tasteful and distinguished cacophony of metal hitting metal. Nothing feels better than relaxing my body to her sensuality - her hedonistic sexuality.

Uranus: one sip; two sips; three sips and four more. She drinks as if there is no tomorrow but down here the winter is everlasting, so maybe the day shall never conquer the night. The night courses on, it engulfs her. She runs her fingers through her hair and that of the man she is caressing with her hips.
"Touch me." Two words yet too open.
He backs away afraid of her needs. She turns to me.
"Kiss me."

Neptune: haunted hearts and fragmented memories. Tonight, in this city, the dead will awake.

Pluto: a love letter to life. A plea to not be forgotten.

We dance away through the darkness.
A beautiful formation; foreign yet so familiar to mankind.
I am the sun.
And we are in orbit.

Night Trains.

I watch the hand counting the seconds on my watch pass sixty. The minute hand ticks into a new position. My mind is dazed, and I can't comprehend what the clock is trying to portray. Is it only midnight? Is it 3am? Is it half past four? The only logical assumption I can make whilst inebriated is that the clock has not yet struck 6am - the night trains are still running.

The wait for a train in the middle of the night is tiresome and the feeling of abandonment is ripe, the passengers who wait with me are just as lost as I am. We all wait patiently, our ears conscious in order to search for the distant noise of electricity - the noise of a train reducing its speed in order to pick us up. Do night trains travel slower in order not to cause an accident between a drunkard and the front of a train? It's as if a spirit possesses me for a split second which urges me to throw myself forwards, onto the tracks. Do I want to be hit by a train? Death is not to be feared, although, it seems death has not come to rob me of my soul tonight - I take a step back.

It's an automatic crave to step back to where I was - over the yellow line - to feel the twisted mix of air rip away at my body, as if the air cannot decide whether it wants to be warm or cold. The throbbing in my head doesn't subdue, nor does the idea to step forwards; the issue is that I don't want to do it alone.

Fear of being alone. Fear of dying alone. Fear of leaving nothing behind. To hear the sweet three words once more, regardless of who it comes from, I'll sacrifice myself in order to hear it. To know that at my funeral, a forgotten friend, an old girlfriend, a distant family member will stand opposite my casket and whisper the blessing made of three words and three syllables.

My left heel rises from the ground; a robotic motion has been launched. *Feel the air. Feel the cold metal. Feel the electricity.*
Let it wake me up. Affection in death is still affection.
There are no circumstances in loving someone whilst they roam this earth and there should be none when they roam the Elysian Fields.

I'm at the edge, I look to my right and can see the headlights from deep in the tunnel. The train has begun to slow down, the screech imminent. There's a thud.
Another man has done it before I can.
His body hits the train and flies in the direction of the tracks.
Screams. Shrieks. Sirens.

I can feel the vomit rise inside. The taste of the acid harsh against the inner surface of my throat. Stumbling around, I make it to a bench as paramedics run around aimlessly.

He's dead.

That could have been me. That was going to be me.

I just wanted to be loved. And so did he.

Slight Smirks.

I watch the high-rise buildings fade into the distance. If this was a movie, my foot would be pressing the pedal of a convertible with the roof down, chords would blare from the speakers, the notes being carried away by the wind that would run through my hair. Alas, I sit on a National Express coach.

Thin, pale and awkward - a figure stands by the vacant seat to my left. It is to reduce discomfiture, that my gaze remains on the woman loading her luggage onto the coach.
A cough - a clearing of the throat or a signal?
"Is this seat free?" Her voice is tender to the ears.
I choke on my words; my self-assurance has plummeted.
"Yeah. Yes, it free."
Tender eyes scan me up and down.
"Thanks."

She takes her place next to me. She is of relatively petite stature yet the fact that she sits with her legs somewhat spread, means she fills her seat and her thigh presses against my own. We watch the final members of a family board the coach and take their seats. The driver makes a few announcements and the car wakes up.

The coach is abruptly alive: the engine, the passengers, and now my heart.

Earphones in, an attempt to distract myself with music is pathetic. What is this sudden need for human interaction I yearn for?
An imitation of the device she used earlier: I cough.
"It's a good day for the beach." In my defence, I seem to have been very ignorant to the fact that I lack the skills to carry out a conversation.
Does she respond out of pity?
"Yeah, that's why I'm off to Brighton. It's time to enjoy this summer." She laughs.
"Last minute plans?" I'm intrigued - she seems so relaxed.
"Yeah. I thought 'fuck it, I'll go Brighton', and now I'm on the coach." Her reposed manner is transfixing.
Slight smirks.

We go the next hour without conference. Instead, we sit, thighs pressed against each other, energies fighting each other, all the while we shake our heads to the beat of our own music. The coach comes to a halt, some of the travellers get off and are replaced by fresher faces.

It's a volley, it's not my turn to start the conversation and so she does.

"What are your plans for today?"
"Well, I'll probably just spend the day at the beach and then walk around." My reply is shaky. I watch a smirk creep upon her face.
"Well, you can always hang out with me."

Slight smirks.

The engine roars, the volume around us rises, and my heart is ablaze.

Constellations.

Broken crescents of hope.
A new constellation being discovered and who
does it form around? Whose shape is it taking?
Hers.
At one point I assumed that Rosie was her own
Cassiopeia. Only now can I conclude that she
was a mere asterism.

There's a moment of pain when I feel that my
feelings for Diana have simply eclipsed those
for Rosie in such a short period of time. I
forgive myself and disregard the pain. The
heartbreak was mutual was it not? We both
wanted this. Didn't we?
Suddenly the silver lining of my heartache
modified itself into a deep red. A torrent of grief
harasses me as I wait the period for my stars to
align once again.

Do my stars align as lonely gases or will they
bond with those belonging to Diana's moons?
An effective attempt to cultivate something
powerful; something so potent that its glow
challenges that of a supernova.

She speaks of her own heartache.
"He was my everything." Sadness is the only
emotion present.
"What happened?"

"He loved someone else." A voice crack. "I thought he would love me forever; I was ready to give him everything." It's almost pathetic the way she says it.

"Maybe he didn't want your everything." I'm taken aback by my own honesty.

"He didn't."

We were both made to mend each other's hearts. In my head, I can see a path; she has been created to teach me what love is.

And I, to teach her life's most fundamental lesson: the ability to fall in and out of love.

Love can be charitable.

Love can be stingy.

It took me one train journey to fall in love with Rosie.

And twelve hours to fall for Diana.

Caller from London.

Dear Diana,

You've put me in the fastest gear.
Hold me tightly please, I must cry these tears.
Take my hand and don't let go.
If we're lovers, please, just say so.

So take me back to one thousand years ago,
Take me back to when we hadn't built these
roads.
Show me what the world would look like if
maybe I had taken things slow.
Do I even know what to say? Or am I just
standing there again? Standing in another
doorway, ready to turn and walk away.

No care and no worries, we don't have any
memories to hold on to forever.
Though I'm still sad because I know hearts will
break and does it mean that all our verses were
fake?
I don't want you to look at me. What will you
see?

Hearts ache every night and minds are ripped
apart.
What went wrong?
Twisted lyrics of our fucked up songs,

Grace the airwaves tonight.

To be held, that's all I wanted from you.
If I wanted more, I would have made more
moves, yet I stayed hidden in the dark.
You tried to wake me up, but I never wanted
you to;
My disposition made me cold-blooded: so cold,
I ran away from you.

Was it even romance?
Or was it merely sex and drug use?
Get high, press those plastic plungers,
The same way I would kiss you.

Created from clay,
Born from individual pains.
Interrupted spurts of devotion,
For we prioritised coition over admiration.

Hearts ache every night and minds are ripped
apart.
What went wrong?
Twisted lyrics of our fucked up songs,
Grace the airwaves tonight.

Human decency means that I can't bring myself
to sign off with the word 'love': lying during a
farewell would be barbaric.
When you go to sleep tonight, forget my voice
and cleanse your air,

And turn the radio off after I've lain my words bare.

Kind regards.

PART THREE:

VIVE LE CHAGRIN.

Watered Tragedies.

No one watches me anymore.
No one pays attention to my shattered
movements.
No one pays attention to the way I attempt to
serenade myself in hopeless affection.
Affection that does not exist.

The current begins to pull me under, wrapping
its tentacles around my ankles, weights linked to
my toes. I am submerged. Any pleas for help
will be muffled by the sound of the harsh waves
above: gravity brings the water to a high crest
and gravity drags me deeper. My arms are
outstretched, ready to push the water out of my
way; alas, I am a mere beat against the rapid
flow - an insult to my state of being - an insult
to my pain.

The view from the water within my
hallucinations is a dramatic landscape. A palace
tower in the distance, a fair maiden by the
window: Diana. She watches me intently, her
hand carefully placing the arrow upon the
platform for rest. An intense grip. She pulls the
bowstring back and I watch the belly vibrate.
From Artemis to Cupid; steal my heart and my
skies.

The tower comes crushing to the ground and I watch the waves engulf the debris. Silence. Not even a whimper, only a deep inhale, a sunken prayer to be taken too.

No one watches me anymore.
No one compliments the way I make the slight attempt to match the colour of my socks to my shirt.
No one compliments the way the way I have decorated my front garden.
Nobody sees my front garden. Nobody comes to visit.

The droplets adorn my face; an intricate pattern upon my forehead, a detailed illustration tattooed onto my cheeks, a minimalistic waterfall down either side of the bridge of my nose. A bewitched finger formed of pins deeply scratches outlines into permanent scars. I turn to face who the hand belongs to and the restrictions to my nerves have me petrified:
"Who am I?"
"Rosalie."

My pageant queen, thick blood cascades down her collagen-filled cheeks, her hair classically styled. My fantasy consort. Each vine develops in a soothing formation, encapsulating my body until I am only a cocoon of regrets, broken hearts and enchanting madness.

"Say you love me."
The tragic statement rapes my memories.

We lived and loved in ruins; both with ruptured hearts and defeated hopes. So lost, so confused, so young: juvenile emotions. I want it back, the electricity we had which I forced my mind to turn off. Was my greatest mistake acting as if what we had was destructive? Seeing things that weren't real? Creating commotions over comments that never truly had any malicious intent? I turned her into the northern line when in reality she ran the tracks from east to west; red coated lines and lips: a direct entrance into the city, past the cages of the heart.

"Do you love me?"
How would I answer that at this moment? It was foolish to leave her but it was also the smartest move I had ever made. I had placed my feelings one step away from being checkmate.

I went from driving down the M11 to breezing down the M23. During the former journey, I drove with the roof up, maybe it would rain; maybe a bird would defecate; maybe the gale winds would blow my hat off.

Love is a woman's creation. Men just try to keep up. This is a woman's creation in a man's world: a world that could not function without the chemistry of thumping hearts and glistening tears. A man's world but ran by women. A man's world but built on the foundation women provide. A man's world but created on the soil of composted rose petals.

Maybe if I keep watering the same spot in my mind, the roses will grow back. What's funny is the fact that I feel as though I never stopped watering the same spot, I just stopped tending to the flowers which is why they died. Now I'm back, wearing only skin on my hands - no gloves - no protection: I welcome the cuts. May the thorns pierce my body in an eloquent fashion if it results in my buds flowering.

As the water begins to wrap around me, I conclude that I am not the last droplet of water falling into the sea of bankrupt fates.
I am the sea.
I am all of them.
And as I begin to fight against the resistance and bring myself up; I break the barrier between watered down tragedies and new beginnings.

And as I float, I notice something resting a few feet away.
I extend my arm: it's too far. The water pities me, a small swash brings the item closer towards me. My fingers grope around until they wrap around something thin, my grip tightens

whilst I place the item on my chest, pain courses
through me.
A single rose.

Raindrops.

"I love you." Standing opposite the mirror panel hung on my wall, I speak to myself nervously. Should my reflection have been identical to Rosie's, I'm sure of the fact that no words would escape me.
Three words carry so much weight that it begins to put me off from saying them. I'm adamant that I've never spoken them to Diana - I could never partake in such a heavy lie - the last person to hear it from me was Rosie: and I hope she wants to hear it again.

"I love you." This time I whisper the words, quiet enough that only my ears are attentive enough to pick up on the distress displayed with the enunciation of each syllable. The air does not respond.
It is a Friday evening; the car of the train is thronged by a mass of office workers on their way home. Once again, I find myself intrigued by the lives of those who I have never come into contact with before.

"Sorry." His briefcase hits my thigh as he cocoons himself in the corner. His handlebar moustache is curled at the tips and he has made a weak attempt to hide his reducing hairline; the sweat-induced shine of his bald head gives it away from the parted gaps of his matt mane.

Suddenly he is all I want to be; to be able to have the confidence to talk to a stranger; to be able to find comfort in the most awkward situations; and when I see the intricate corrugated wedding band positioned on his finger, all I want is to be able to go home to somebody.

The train calls at Holborn and I watch him get off with great haste.

The train car would have been more beneficial to me should it have been empty; nobody else seems to be leaving an impact, thus they merely steal and swallow the air that I long for. I wait the prolonged seconds till I reach my stop and address the robotic remarks blaring from the speakers with concealed joy.

The ability to navigate through Tottenham Court Road during peak time makes a man immune to any forms of physical hurt: being stabbed by the tip of a Fulton umbrella; having your shoulder blade smacked by a commuter running for the next train; and having the piercing shrieks of a wailing child trimming every nerve in your body. Alas, it does not grant you resistance to the automatic torture felt when a couple display their affection for each other on the Northern Line platform.

It's amusing how watching others do the same thing that I once did myself brings an acidic vomit to make its way around my body. Am I jealous? Or am I just uncomfortable? All the other commuters observe with faces of both distaste and awe as both continue to absorb each other. I shift my gaze away as do many others. There is a shared appreciation and respect we have for the couple though I don't know what it is until I step onto the tightly crammed train heading north: it's their bravery.

Rosalie and I would struggle to hold hands in public vicinities – perhaps the blame falls on me.
"What if someone sees?" The question must have caused her eternal pain, did she question whether or not I was embarrassed by her. Did she wonder whether I did not want to be seen with her? Did I?
It's only now, as we random strangers swing from left to right whilst we pass Mornington Crescent, do I deduce that I wasn't humiliated by being Rosie's man – I was discomposed by the idea that others may see me as weak.

The words of my father come back to me, flooding my memory. It's similar to leaving the faucet running in the bathroom as it slowly fills; the water begins to escape the room and trickle down through the cracks until the water damages the whole house. The extended years that I have tried to remove him from my cache have proven to be a failure. The way his voice would crack at random moments and the fury behind every statement he'd make.

I don't want to hear it. Nonetheless, I have to.

"Love was not made for the weak man."

Natural instinct causes me to let go of the pole and brings me crashing against the door, slamming my chin against the window. *I didn't want to hear it.* If I had replayed the scene correctly, it would have ended with my father proceeding to emasculate me.

"You little shit." Rancour of high dosage inoculated his speech.

I want to pound against the doors to open: to feel the air penetrate my follicles whilst I stand in the darkness of the tunnel.

No one can hear my heavy breathing.

No one can see me shed my first tear of the night.

No one notices me.

When my feet meet the slabs of the platform, I break out into a run.

"Move." Odd turns are made in bid to get to the front.

The icy exterior of the raindrops harasses me and cause the pavements and roads to become a surface of caution.

Arrest me for jaywalking but don't arrest me for chasing the covet of my bosom.

There is an alleyway in Belsize Park where the younger residents dwell; apartments are fractionally cheaper and the view is somewhat more dull, yet it remains one of the most enthralling locations known to man. And as I stand in the centre of the alley, surrounded by coloured doors, my emotions begin to burn their way through my veins. I didn't know how I felt back then, but I know how I feel now and take great pleasure in recognising that no longer am I too reserved to prove that I love her. I hold my torch high: visible for all of humanity.

The yellow door swings open: a man steps out followed by a woman in a green coat. The skies begin to come crashing down. My journey becoming a waste.
"I love you." I mouth the words, not even a whimper escapes me.

Before she can pull apart her gaze from the man she embraces with her lips, I turn on my heel and quicken my pace.
I lost her then. I've lost her now.
Goodbye my sweet rose.
Goodbye my sweet Rosalie.

Little Venice.

No answers, only questions fill my mind.
What will she say?
What will I say?
Who is he?
The latter interrogative statement clouds my
judgements.

I want to say that she's moved on too fast but
then again, I did too. Mentally preparing myself,
I bring the water to my mouth and allow it to
saturate my tongue. What is she doing at this
very moment? Is she as nervous as I am?

Our brief conversation over text began when I
received a message out of the blue last night.
Reading the name of the sender made me feel
like I was drowning; imagine a pearl slowly
drifting to the bottom of the seabed when it
should have come to the water surface - my
spirits should have risen. Instead, I ignored the
message and decided to respond later, after
thoroughly drafting a rejoinder.

She wanted to meet up and I agreed. Now, as I
sit on the 205 bus towards Paddington whilst
making wordless prayers, I have a revelation. A
sign from the higher power that it is time to let
go - my nerves gradually subdue.

Today, in order to release the wrongdoings that plague me, stating my regrets must be delivered. I can drink and get high - waste my days into an abyss - however to not be able to swallow my pride and make an apology will make me a man of no honour. When they find my exanimate body on the tartan sofa in my studio, to have them find a man of integrity and love is my final prayer.

The phone in my pocket vibrates. I turn it off: a plea for the world to be silent.

When my eyes focus on her for what may be the last time, I analyse each part of her. My irises analyse her every movement: the way she walks with one foot directly in front of the other; the way her arms don't swing, making it seem like she has great posture; the way her ears rise slightly when she smiles. Her little black dress bares her legs which glow bronze with fake tan and natural sunlight; her lips are painted red indication of the blood she will spill when she bites into my heart; her pumps are coloured a vivid yellow - a warning sign for me to stay in my place.

"Hello." The sweet flavour of candy no longer seems distasteful.
"Hi." The nervous shake in my voice that is expected does not present itself.

As we sit in the floating café of a petit crimson boat on the Grand Union Canal. The discussion begins with apologies for the pains and the sorrows that we have both caused each other. She seems so proud of the development my character has been through yet still seems so upset over the decision that I have made. And I, myself, am so glad that she has found somebody who can plant the seeds and grow the flowers of a future generation. It would be selfish of me to hold her to the words she once said during the times in which we sliced each other open, with blades sharpened with vile curses.

His name is Matthew. He works as a data analyst for a large bank in the city. He's soft-natured and intelligent: the attributes that I lacked. They have been in contact for a few weeks now. They met through friends; friends we once shared though, left me when Rosie and I parted. I am not bitter nor am I jealous, nonetheless grief washes over me.

We buy another coffee to share between us both, such an intimate activity: kissing the same lid of the woman whose heart I broke. It is not only a drink yet the ability to also see our hurts through the eyes of each other. I made mistakes nevertheless, she did too; so to stand here and say that I alone am the reason for our demise would be foolish. I alone did not have the power to cause anything - I am weak.

As the time treads on, we speak little; nonetheless, our shared eye contact writes stories longer and more impactful than Tolstoy's. We are authors of dual heartbreak. Our novels share so much in common: both unreliable narrators and both the victim of sad kismets.

The boat shakes: a siren that our time together has truly come to a close. To keep her on this boat longer would be an act of harbouring her from floating on the river of future glee.

"Goodbye." Summer lollies and luxury creams melt under the heat of my loss.
"Goodbye."
Have we promised to stay friends? I do not know. What I do know, is that it is time for me to release myself from the link of this tortuous chain.
She looks back at me - pity in her eyes - vivid behind the violet layer that has formed.
"I promise," Promise what? What has she sworn to? "I promise that I'll always be there for you."

And as we part ways, I understand every slightest action that occurred over the past few

months. Starting to appreciate the intricacies
that this universe has gifted me, I am grateful: I
am thankful for Rosalie, thankful for Diana, and
thankful for the way that when we separate and
go about our different journeys we will
experience varying emotions.
I will ignore the scrubbers and loiterers of the
moored boats; not due to fear, rather so I can
cherish the optimism that is brushed into the
feathers of the ducks.

Broken boats and broken leaves.
Little Venice still holds my dreams.
Orla, Carys, Rosalie and Diana,
Anchored to the river,
No longer anchored to my future.

Foreign Souls.

Lost souls roam the dance floors.
Every step they make a scream to free
themselves of tragedies.
They'll do anything to make sure their heart rate
soars.
No kisses. No physical pleasures. Only plungers
being pressed in tune with the melodies.

"Lasciami andare." The lady in brown mumbles
to the memory of her ex-lover. She pleads for
the image of his body to leave her; to let her
move on.
"Ich möchte bei dir bleiben." His shirt clenched
in his hand, being used as a rag to wipe the
perspiration that is leaking from his body. He
wails in pain as he injects more morphine. It is
not the opiate that brings him to this state, nor
the piercing of the skin; it is the fact that what
he has spent years trying to forget, wants to
cling to him a little longer.

An abundance of languages. A profusion of
devastation.

"Ce sont des imbéciles.
La douleur ne quitte pas une personne, la
sensation se cache simplement." He is older
than the rest of us who lie strewn across the

numbing tiles. He is wiser. He is a man of importance - evident from his hidden face.
I nod and instinctively lean forwards for him to ignite the end of my spliff.
He cups my chin and brings his lighter closer, the flame illuminates his face. Every one of his features are so familiar, notwithstanding, still alien to my mind.

As the smoke clouds the room and our bodies begin to fade into oblivion, I make one last call to the outside world.
"Who are you?" I scream at the elderly gentleman.
"Je suis toi," A Chelsea smile. "I am you."
Nihility tries to swallow me, I don't allow it to.

Running: the only activity that makes sense in any situation. My feet pound against the floor until I'm out of the room and under the city lights. *Where are the stars?* The clouds of pollution shield my view of Gaea's construction.

Do I want to be found lifeless in a club?
Do I want to be found on a drug-fuelled high?
No.
I want to be found. I really do.

But I don't want to be found as a disordered man - I want to be found as a man - just a man.

Let me inter my story in a tomb far away: in a tomb guarded until others can understand my depression; in a tomb blanketed with roses.

Let me bury my legacy somewhere far from the location that caused my internal destruction. To leave London is to leave life itself. Must I pluck my very own soul to cleanse my body of previous aches? Yes: therefore, I must take off. I must plant my legacy under an aurora, north of this city in which heartbreak prevails.

Sorrows flood the land of this earth, seeping through the pores of the soil. Regardless of its concentration, it lacks the potency to dilute the lava of love.

Love is eternal.

Should two lovers have their souls plucked from this cold world, their love shall always remain.

Should two lovers have their relationship ripped away, their love shall always remain.

A legacy of passion.

A legacy of love.

One-way Train.

Three options: one-way, return, open return.
A long pause. What are my plans?
A sign flashes on the screen signifying that my
session will terminate if I do not pick an
option.
My index finger presses down firmly on the
screen: *one-way*.

The continuous murmur of travellers
conversing, restaurants preparing food and
tickets printing permeate the air. It is much too
loud. Groping the receipt slot, I pluck my tickets
out with an unconcerned aura radiating from
me. The location was chosen at random, that
way it shall hurt less when circumstances turn
sour. To be raised in life under the guise that
you must have a plan, should be a sin or maybe
it is God's alternative form of punishment.
Human ignorance caters to it: we set our minds
to a task and we trial all we can do in order to
achieve it; the fact that our failures will bring
the blade down are forgotten in times of
adventure. Though tonight, I recall this fact and
remember the hidden truth of our universe.

My train leaves in ten minutes and to say that I
am nervous would be an understatement of my
feelings. Quickly packing my sandwich and

packet of Kettle crisps in a plastic bag, I make my way with hurried steps to platform five.

The platform is undisturbed – the noise of the main station centre having been tranquilised. It also seems barren.

"Rather quiet, innit?" The ticket officer seems like a man crafted of a mellow personality.

"Yeah." One word that should be interpreted as three: *leave me alone*.

"They will get on later, so you won't have an empty train to yourself." A rather distasteful joke, regardless, I flash a smile to be polite.

"Most likely at York or Newcastle." The bile in my throat thickens at the sound of Newcastle. It seems that no matter what I do to get away from her - the idea of her - she comes rushing back to me.

"Newcastle is nice." That statement may be incorrect for I've never been, I only know it through the pictures Rosalie's words would print in my mind. The officer agrees with me and we continue our pointless conversation for a minute longer.

I have no luggage to load onto the train and so I say farewell to the man whom I have already grown fond of. I take the backpack that weighs me down and place it by my side as I take my seat by the window.

The lady opposite reads a book on Greek mythology with the figure of Athena coating the cover. The child behind me complains that his soup is cold. "Well maybe if you had eaten it earlier like I said-", his mother's voice is harsh yet glazed with care. The elderly man a few rows in front clutches his Bearded Collie puppy in his lap after it has run itself tired around the car. We're an odd grouping nonetheless over the first few minutes, our silence and our auras become so familiar. Naturally, the dynamic alters as passengers get off and new people step on.

It calls for Newcastle. I push my earphones in deep - a vain attempt to shield myself from hearing the accent that would bring me to life, the mourning period is not yet over.

I'll be at Edinburgh soon and my five-hour journey will have been complete. Five hours prescribed for reflection and resolutions. What will I do now? Will I stay in Edinburgh? Will I go back to London? The possibilities are infinite however, the realities are surgically decided.

The fear begins to kick in. What have I done? *Go back to her. Plead for her love.* No, she deserves to move on. The worst feeling is coming to terms with the fact that real value is only discovered when value had been misplaced.

When the train calls at its final stop, I stand petrified.
"Need help?" Her accent is thick but beautiful.
"Yes please." I grasp her hand as she assists me off the train and onto the platform. It's not an instantaneous release and I cherish the unnecessary three extra seconds that I held her hand - a form of self-assurance.
We don't ask for each other's names; everything that is meant to be said is delivered in the form of a mutual twinkle in our eyes.

It's a lonely world.
Though now I recognise that there are more hands to hold onto.

Soft Wails.

The arms of thousands of broken-hearted fools
outstretched across rivers, seas and oceans, all
making a final effort to hold onto the anchor of
affection.
We all sit on benches, ledges and staircase steps,
staring at a delineate landscape that our
imagination delicately sketches of our fractured
kismets.

"Say you won't let go." I whimper, holding the
hands of the men and women of France,
Ethiopia, Australia and the other 192 countries
that configure humanity.
Mythical surfaces of millions of hands link to
form a chain around our universe. Suns break
free into supernovas and moons float away from
structured orbit, yet our chain never breaks.
Each hand, each person, each heart: a barrier to
protect our solar system. To protect ourselves.

But far in the distance where the solo star of
another galaxy glows bright against a blank
black background, we watch attentively. Hope.
The only omnipotent cell that cruises through
our blood streams. Our bodies so alive with
aspiration that we cling to the cornucopias
nearby. And as I blow with pursed lips into the
mouthpiece, I watch as rose petals erupt from
the bell. A finale fit for my deepest affair.

We stand with redemption at the tip of our fingers.

"Reach for me." A voice like treacly figs, freshly plucked from a springtime tree.

I turn to face her. Am I expecting to see 'ma donna' adorned with a crimson petal diadem pinned to her hair? Who do I expect to see?

I stretch my arm a little further, a burning sensation runs up my muscles.

"Hold me," I whisper, the salty water starting their journey down my hollow cheeks. "And never let go."

"I promise."

The thorny stems that were once so tightly wound around my eyes begin to relax and the pain subdues as I open them wide.

There she stands - my hand enclosed in her own - standing upon the dishevelled body of Phobos.

"Elpis?" Her nod translates that I have correctly identified her.

"I won't let go."

We stand alone - just the two of us - against the backdrop of an unforeseen future.

"I promise."

I'm testing to hold on to a world that no longer belongs to me. It's a coming of age occasion, from naive to sophisticated. Do I want to let go?

If I do; I will no longer remember the individual notes of each of my troubles - I shall only hold memory of the songs I've composed over the antecedent years.

Elpis tries staying true to her word, having said that, it is I who cannot hold on tight enough.
Serene smiles.
Shattered hearts.
Soft wails.
I have no water left in my body to cry this pain away.
"Much love." Impetuous whispers.
The darkness will swallow me whole and I shall receive it with felicity. No more time to contemplate.

Ne me lâche pas.
Don't let go.
Seulement je peux me libérer.
Only I can free myself.

I let go.

Acknowledgements

Fireflies in the City was the first 'longer' piece of work that I ever completed. It was also the first piece of creative writing that I managed to focus on without drifting.

I know that I will be forever indebted to the people in my life who have helped shape this collection along the way. So firstly, a round of applause for my parents and two sisters (Samiha and Nafisa) who inspired the core theme of this collection: strength.

Fiction writing allows you to draw from your own emotions and experiences – experiences that would have never happened without my little group of friends. Therefore, I would like to thank Alec, Ilham, Mel, Sadi and Zoya; who have not been in my life for long and may not stay forever but have been fundamental in opening my eyes to the world. They've also been the ones who read through my individual pieces and gave their feedback (always kind but constructive too).

I started writing this collection on 3rd January 2020 when I got on the 25 bus at Stratford and I finished it on 13th March after a trip walking down the canal around Maida Vale. A three-month period in which I learnt so much about myself and my ability to cope with new things. For that reason, I am forever thankful for living in London: with its grey ceiling, congested roads, oddly shaped skyline, and its thousands of commuters who I like to assign fictional backstories to.

Not only am I indebted to family, friends, and the city, but also to all of my English teachers. To E. Champion who first gave me *The Catcher in the Rye* to read and introduced me to the idea of coming-of-age; who if it weren't for, I would have never decided to keep reading. To Katy Thompson and Tejal Shah who helped me grow my passion for writing. To Damian Stanford-Harris, who changed my life by introducing me to the works of Fitzgerald through *The Great Gatsby*. And a huge thanks to both Clara Gormley and Steven Quincey-Jones for reading and critique this collection of stories.

The only reason I even had the confidence to try self-publish was due to the support of Esther Pearce (whose degree in English came in handy during edits) and James Kane – both amazingly kind and helpful.

In conclusion, to my family, friends, teachers, mentors, and my city: I am forever grateful.

And to my readers: thank you.

Ariq was born and raised in London.

Always creative, he enjoys watching films, writing (articles, short stories, and screenplays), and painting.

He is currently working on a novel and magazine website.

He is also a student.

Find him on Instagram: ariq_1350

Printed in Great Britain
by Amazon

47437811R00061